THE

"This is one of those stories you [...] *problem with The Visible Filth* [...] *some of this imagery will rise, then stick around even when you close your eyes. So go on, open this book up. You won't be forgetting it any time soon."*

STEPHEN GRAHAM JONES, AUTHOR OF THE ELVIS ROOM

"Ballingrud is a powerful, mesmerizing writer, and The Visible Filth proves he can frighten with the best of them. If I weren't already jealous of what he can do, I would be now."

SIMON STRANTZAS, AUTHOR OF BURNT BLACK SUNS

"Ballingrud is a master at writing about the darkness inside us. And as terrifying as it might be to see, you can't look away or close your eyes against it thanks to his beautifully precise and evocative prose. There's a dark heart to The Visible Filth and Ballingrud uses its blood for ink to tell a story that really gets under your skin, or rather calls to something that might already be there. Fantastic work, highly recommended."

RAY CLULEY, AUTHOR OF WATER FOR DROWNING

"Thoroughly unsettling. Ballingrud knows exactly how to crawl his way under your skin."

DREAD CENTRAL

"By witnessing, we become complicit. In Nathan Ballingrud's unsettling and captivating novella, The Visible Filth, a simple act, a bit of curiosity, turns into something much darker—a poison that seeps into our flesh, unable to look away, a plague brought forth, the page becoming our undoing."

RICHARD THOMAS, AUTHOR OF DISINTEGRATION

"If you didn't gag while reading The Visible Filth, you're a tougher man than I. Ballingrud's cautionary tale of what happens when you stick your nose where it doesn't belong will stick with you for a long, long time."

ROBB OLSON, BOOKED. PODCAST

"Deeply sinister, potent and grotesque."

RJ BAYLEY, POPCORN HORROR

"This isn't the type of horror you can easily categorize, put inside a box and say, 'THIS. This is what makes this story scary.' The Visible Filth is deeply unnerving and you're not sure why. It has all the requisite thrills and chills, but it's what's under the surface that will be your undoing."

JOSHUA CHAPLINSKY, LITREACTOR.COM

A This Is Horror Publication
www.ThisIsHorror.co.uk

ISBN: 978-0-9575481-9-0

First published in Great Britain in 2015 by This Is Horror

Editor-in-Chief: Michael Wilson
Deputy Editor: Dan Howarth
Cover and Design: Pye Parr

Printed in Great Britain

THE
VISIBLE
FILTH

NATHAN
BALLINGRUD

THIS IS
HORROR

THE ROACHES WERE in high spirits. There were half a dozen of them, caught in the teeth of love. They capered across the liquor bottles, perched atop pour spouts like wooden ladies on the prows of sailing ships. They lifted their wings and delicately fluttered. They swung their antennae with a ripe sexual urgency, tracing love sonnets in the air.

Will, the bartender on duty, stood watching them, with his back to the rest of the bar. He couldn't move. He was bound by a sense of obligation to remain where he was, but the roaches stirred a primordial revulsion in him, and the urge to flee was palpable. His flesh shivered in one convulsive movement.

He worked the six PM to two AM shift at Rosie's Bar, a little hole-in-the-wall tucked back in the maze of streets of uptown New Orleans, surrounded by shotgun houses settling into their final repose, their porches bedazzled in old Mardi Gras beads and sprung couches. The bar's interior reflected its environment: a few tables and chairs against the back wall, a jukebox, ranks of stools against the bar. He often had the misfortune of minding the place when the roaches started feeling passionate. It happened a few times a year, and each time it paralyzed him with horror.

At the moment, his only customers were Alicia: a twenty-eight year old server at an oyster bar in the French Quarter, a long-time regular, and his best friend; and Jeffrey: her boyfriend of the moment, soon to be hustled into the ranks of the exes, if Will knew her at all. Jeffrey was one of those pretty boys with the hair and the lashes she liked, but he was not on her wavelength at all. Will gave him another month, tops.

"This place is disgusting," Alicia said, watching the show from a somewhat safer distance.

"Don't slam the bar, babe," said Jeffrey. "It's just bugs."

"Fucking gross bugs who want to get busy on my bottle of Jameson."

Will just nodded. It was, indeed, disgusting.

"You should get an exterminator, brother," said Jeffrey. "Seriously."

The same conversation every time. Just different faces. "Yup. Talk to the boss."

"You know they say when you see one, there's thousands more in the walls."

"Oh yeah? Is that what they say?"

Alicia said, "Shut up, Jeffrey."

"Make me."

She pulled his face to hers and kissed him deeply. Apparently love was in the air at Rosie's Bar that night. Jeffrey cupped the back of her head with one hand and let the other go sliding up her leg. He was a good boy. He knew what to do.

Will waited for the roach to relinquish its claim to the Jameson, then poured himself a shot. People from Louisiana liked to call the cockroach the official state bird; they were practically everywhere, and you couldn't worry too much if you saw one. No matter how clean you kept your place, they were going to get in. But when you got something like this, you were infested. There must be a huge nest somewhere in the wall, or underneath the building. Maybe more than one. He didn't think an exterminator would fix this problem. The whole wall needed to be torn out. Maybe the whole building would have to be burned down to the dark earth, and then you'd have to keep on burning, all the way down to their mother nests in Hell.

The roaches made little ticking noises as they scrambled about, and he had the brief, uncanny certainty that the noises would cohere into a kind of language if he listened carefully enough.

After a few more minutes, the bugs retired to their bedrooms, and the rows of bottles resumed their stately, lighted beauty. Jeffrey had his hand in Alicia's shirt.

"That shirt comes off, and it's free drinks all night," Will said.

Jeffrey pulled away, his face flushed. Alicia smoothed her shirt and her hair. "You wish, child."

"I really do."

Alicia circled her finger over the bar. "Shots. Line 'em up. Maybe you'll see something before the night is through."

He doubted it, but he poured them anyway.

Like most 24-hour bars in New Orleans, the place did a decent business even on off nights. Most of the late night clientele was made up of service industry drones like Alicia and Jeffrey, or cab drivers, or prostitutes, or just the lonely losers of the world, sliding their rent dollar by dollar into the video poker machines lined up like totems against the back wall.

A few college kids filed in, finding a table some distance from the bar. After a moment one of them broke away and approached Will with an order for the table. Will cast his eye across the bunch: three girls and two guys, including the one placing the order. Almost certainly some of them were underage. College kids usually hit the Quarter for fun, but the Loyola campus was just a few blocks away, so inevitably a few of them drifted into Rosie's throughout the week, looking for a quiet night.

"Everybody twenty-one?" Will said.

The kid showed him his ID, sighing with the patience of a beleaguered saint. Legal less than a month.

"What about everybody else?"

"Yeah, man. Want me to get them?"

A weak bluff. Will thought about it; it was a Tuesday night, the shift was almost over, and the drawer was light. He decided he didn't care. "Don't worry about it."

Someone put some money into the jukebox and Tom Waits filled the silence. The college kids huddled around the table once they got their drinks, their backs forming a wall against the world. They seemed to be fixated on something between them. They were a lot quieter than he thought they'd be, though, which he considered a blessing. The night continued along its smooth course until Eric and his buddies walked in, staining the mood. They'd obviously already been on the bar circuit that night, coming in with beers in hand, descending on the pool table. Eric lifted his chin to Will in greeting; his three friends didn't trouble themselves.

"Hey Eric. You guys need anything?"

"We're set for now, brother. Thanks."

Eric was a little plug of muscle and charisma. He was the sweetest guy in the world when sober. When he was drunk, though, every human interaction became a potential flashpoint for violence. He lived in an apartment above the bar, so Will got to see that side of him a lot.

"How's Carrie?" Alicia asked, drawing him back.

Will shrugged, feeling a surge of unanchored guilt. "She's fine I guess. Head in the computer all the time, working on that paper she's doing for school. Same as always."

"You got yourself a smart one."

Jeffrey perked up, caught in a wash of inspiration. "Hey, we should all go out sometime. Does she like football? We could go to a Saints game."

The idea almost made him laugh. "No, man, she doesn't like football."

Alicia touched his hand. "That's totally a good idea though. Let's just hang out. I haven't seen her in weeks. We could double date!"

"Oh my God."

"Don't be a dick, Will. Make it happen."

"I'll suggest it to her. I'm telling you, though, she's living her school work right now. I'm not even sure she remembers my name."

"Make it happen."

A bottle shattered somewhere by the pool table, followed by a muffled grunt. The bar went silent except for the sound of scuffling shoes and short bursts of breath, overlaid with a jaunty dirge from The Violent Femmes. Eric and one of the guys he'd come in with were grappled together, Eric's arm around the other guy's neck. He hit him in the face with three quick shots. The guy gripped the jagged neck of his beer bottle and swung it around to rake it across Eric's arm. Blood splashed to the grungy linoleum.

"Goddamnmit!" Will said. "Somebody get that fucking bottle!"

Nobody wanted to get near them. One of the other guys Eric had come in with, some heavily muscled punk with his hat on backwards and some kind of Celtic tattoo snaking down his right arm, leaned against the pool table and laughed. "God *damn*, son," he said.

Fights happened all the time, and sometimes you just had to let them play themselves out, but the jagged bottle elevated this to a higher level of calamity.

Eric wouldn't let go of the guy's neck. He hit him again a few more times, and when the bottle came around once more he took it on the cheek. Blood sprayed onto the floor, the pool table, across his own face. Eric made a high-pitched noise that seemed to signal a transition into another state of being, that seemed to carve this moment from the rational world and hold it separate. It seemed that another presence had entered the room, something invisible, some blood-streaked thing crawling into the light.

Jeffrey flew in from the sidelines, like some berserker canary in a sky full of hawks. He threw himself against them both, wrapping his weak little hands around the wrist of the guy with the broken bottle. The momentum of his charge carried them all into the table where the college kids were sitting, and everybody went down in a clamor of toppling chairs and spilling glasses and shrieks of fear.

Alicia shouted something, running toward the tumble of bodies. Will rounded the bar – too late, he knew, he should have been the one to engage them – and followed her into the scrum. A bright flash leapt from the tangle of bodies, like lightning in the belly of a thunderhead.

By the time he arrived, it was already over. Eric had maneuvered on top of the other guy and was giving him a brutal series of jabs to the side of the head before somebody finally pulled him off. His antagonist, deprived of his weapon, moved groggily, his eyes already swelling shut, his face a bloodied wreck. His right hand looked broken. The kids who'd been at the table formed a penumbra around the scene, looking on with an almost professional calm.

One of the girls said, "Did you call the police?"

"Of course I fucking did."

She looked at the others and said, "Let's go." They dispersed immediately, pouring through the door and sublimating into the night.

Once freed from the actual entanglement, Eric had grown immediately calm, like a chemical rendered inert. The flesh on his cheek was torn in a gruesome display; it would leave a scar that would pull his whole face out of alignment. He seemed not to feel it. His eyes were dilated and unfocused, but the rage seemed spent, and he went back to the pool table to retrieve what was left of his beer.

"Eric," Will said. "You need to get to a hospital. Seriously."

"Cops are coming?" he said. The words were a slush in his mouth.

"Yes."

"Fucking pussy." Will didn't know if that was meant for him or the guy on the floor. "All right, come on," Eric said, and headed out the door. His remaining friends followed, not sparing a glance for their vanquished comrade.

Will, Alicia, and Jeffrey were left with the beaten man, who was only now pulling himself with glacial slowness into the closest upright chair. Will fetched a bar rag and gave it to him for his face, but he just held it limply, his hand suspended at his side. A thin stream of blood drooled from a cut on his face and pooled in a wrinkle on his shirt.

"You all right, man?"

"Just fuck off, dude."

"Yeah, you can say that to the cops, too, asshole." It was easy to be tough when the danger had passed. He felt a little ashamed by it, but not enough to shut himself up. "Grabbing a bottle in a fight is chickenshit."

The guy stood abruptly, knocking his chair over. Will felt his stomach lurch; he'd badly miscalculated the scene, and now he was going to pay for it with his own broken teeth. But the guy didn't waste any attention on him. He tottered briefly, achieved his bearings, and headed out the front door, into the warm night air. They watched him walk slowly down the sidewalk, into the lightless neighborhood, until he was obscured by parked cars and trees.

"What the hell was that?" Alicia said. Will turned to offer up some wry commentary about Eric and his friends, but saw right away that the question was for Jeffrey, not him. "What did you think you were doing?"

"I don't know," Jeffrey said. "It was instinct, I guess."

"You're not some tough guy. You could have been seriously hurt."

"I know. But he had a broken bottle. He could have killed him."

Will had no stomach for listening to Jeffrey play the humble hero. He had a sudden urge to break a chair over his head. "You did good," he said.

Only now did he notice how much blood there was, all over his bar, like strange little sigils. On the green felt of the pool table, on the floor beside it, splashed on the chairs and pooled in a little puddle where the guy had been sitting just moments before. Stipples and coins of it making a trail over the floor where Eric had walked. A smear of it on the glass door, left there when he'd pushed his way out. Rosie's Bar felt curiously hollow, like a socket from which something had been torn loose, or a voided womb.

Still no sign of the police. On a fucking Tuesday night. What else could they be doing?

The three of them spent the next twenty minutes restoring the tables and chairs to their places, wiping up as much of the blood as they could find. Will found a smartphone against the back wall, probably dropped there by one of the college kids when their table was knocked into. He slid it into his pocket while he finished cleaning.

When they were done, he returned to his place behind the bar and poured himself a shot of Jameson. He knocked it down and poured three more, arrayed them on the bar, one for each.

They raised their glasses and touched the rims. His hand was shaking.

"To New Orleans!" Alicia said.

"This fucking town."

They drank.

*   *   *

WILL LIKED COMING home in the small hours. Carrie always left the light over the oven on for him before going to bed, creating a little island of domestic warmth: the clean white range, the fat green teapot, the checkered hand towel hanging from the oven door. Everything else was an ocean of quiet darkness. He set his keys softly on the countertop, retrieved a bottle of Abita Amber from the fridge, and settled down at the kitchen table. He'd given himself a buzz at the bar, and the world seemed pleasantly muddled to him now, not unlike the feeling of being half-asleep on a late morning.

He tried to push the fight out of his mind. The police finally did stroll in, well after Alicia and Jeffrey had gone home and Doug, the graveyard bartender, had taken over. Will had waited for them with growing impatience, nursing a beer in the corner. When they arrived, they took his statement, gave the place a cursory look, and ambled out again, looking fairly unimpressed by it all. Which was all to the good. Nobody wanted on-duty cops hanging out in the bar. Just having the squad car parked out front – pale white in the dark, the reflective NOPD lettering on the doors flaring into a bright blue warning in the headlights of every passing car – was murder on business. When Will headed home, the bar had been empty, and Doug was leaned back against the counter, reading yesterday's newspaper.

This fight was Eric's worst; he'd taken real damage from that broken bottle. Surely this would slow him down just a little bit. At the very least, it might keep him from drinking while he waited for the stitches to heal. The thought brought Will some peace. He'd make a point of dropping in on him the next day, to make sure he'd wised up and gone to the emergency room.

Feeling restless, he wandered through the living room, navigating the darkness by muscle memory, and opened the door into the bedroom. Carrie was asleep, the sheets kicked down around her ankles in the heat. She ended up knocking half the covers to the floor every night, but couldn't sleep with the air conditioner on because it made her too cold. It was a battle Will had long ago surrendered, having resigned himself to making do with the weak cooling effort of the ceiling fan. She was wearing a t-shirt emblazoned with Captain America's shield, hiked up around her waist, revealing a pair of white granny-panties which, once, he had found both odd and charming. Her short blond hair was rucked up against the pillow, and her face had the defenseless, wide-open innocence of deep sleep. It was easiest to love her when she was like this. He touched her cheek, hooked a strand of hair back over her ear.

He stood there for a moment, trying to decide if he was tired enough to join her. But the clangor of the evening still rang in his blood. He went back to the kitchen and grabbed another beer from the fridge.

A faint musical chime sounded somewhere, far away: a descending spill of notes in a minor key, like a refrain from gloomy lullaby. He stopped in mid-stoop, the cold air from the refrigerator washing over him. There was nothing more, so he brought his beer back to the kitchen table and settled into his chair.

The sound came again, and this time he felt a vibration in his pants pocket. It was the cell phone from the bar, the one left behind by someone in that crowd of kids. He slipped it free and examined it: a bright yellow smartphone, fairly new judging by its condition, with a series of sparkling heart stickers affixed to its outer rim. The desktop was a picture of some far eastern mountain, snow-capped, radiant with reflected sunlight. He slid his finger across the screen to access the display, and there was a notification of two text messages received.

A momentary hesitation flickered through his mind before he looked at them. Privacy be damned; she should have been more careful if she didn't want him to look.

The messages were from somebody named Garrett:

I think something is in here with me.

And then, sent two minutes later: *I'm scared.*

Will put the phone down and dropped his hands, staring at it. The fog in his head dissipated somewhat, and he was surprised to feel his heart beating. The screen remained lit for a few seconds, and then blinked back to its inert state. He sat silently, unsure of what to do next. A sporadic ticking sounded somewhere in the darkness, beyond his little island of light. A scuttling roach. The phone chimed again, vibrating raucously against the tabletop. He leaned over and looked at the message.

It knows I'm here. It's trying to talk. Please come.

"What the fuck," Will whispered. He picked up the phone and scrolled up through Garrett's messages. Maybe this was a game. Maybe they went back to the bar, knew he had the phone, and were fucking with him. Before these texts, there were only six messages exchanged between them. Arranging a study session for class, a mention of coffee; simple banalities. Nothing like this.

They were messing with him. He texted a reply: *You can pick up the phone tomorrow night at the bar. I go in at six.* Send.

Enough time passed that he figured it was all over. He took another pull from his beer and decided it was just about time to join Carrie in bed after all. The roach scuttled somewhere over toward the cabinets, but his normal sense of revulsion was dimmed by his weariness, and his irritation at the events of the night. To his own surprise, his brain kept cycling around to Jeffrey. Again and again. Launching himself into the fray and maybe tipping the balance in Eric's favor. The look in Alicia's eyes afterwards: she'd said she was pissed, and she probably was a little, but there was a heat in that look that did not come from anger. It made Will feel small.

The phone clamored again, making him jump. "God damn you," he said to it, and picked it up to see what it had to say.

Tina?

He sighed and texted back, against his own better judgment. *No, not Tina, asswipe. I have her phone.* He pressed send, and immediately felt a swelling of guilt. Why the hostility? Maybe the guy really didn't know.

Who are you? Get Tina.

She left it at the bar. I'm the bartender. Tell her to pick it up tomorrow night. And stop fucking around. Send.

He shut the ringer off, and set it on the dishtowel from the stove, to dull its vibrations. It sat there, a cheery yellow rectangle in the dark cave of his kitchen. He finished off the beer, trying to keep his mind unanchored, free-floating; but Jeffrey and Alicia kept bobbing to the surface, thwarting his efforts. He imagined them entangled together in bed, a pale twist of limbs and sweat. Something dark turned over inside him, and he felt the sting of shame prickle his skin.

The scuttling sound intensified, and the roach veered into the light. It froze there, as if realizing its error. Its antennae searched the air, trying to gauge the severity of its predicament. Will considered the effort involved in getting up to kill it; it would be long gone before he even got close. He stomped his foot, trying to scare it. The roach did not flinch, brash as a rooster, unmoved by the sudden trembling of the world beneath it.

The phone vibrated quietly on its dishtowel. Will didn't even bother to look at it. He got up from the table, placing the empty beer bottles into the recycling bin with a muted clink, and headed to bed. The roach disappeared under the refrigerator. Everything was clean, orderly, and quiet.

WHEN HE AWOKE, Carrie was already up, and the smell of coffee and frying bacon floated into the bedroom like a summons from God. He lay in the sweet fog of half sleep, relishing the bliss of it. He listened to Carrie's footsteps as she moved around in the kitchen, listened to her hum something quietly to herself, and felt a surprising well of gratitude for this fine life. He imagined Eric waking up in whatever grim hovel he'd retreated to last night, his face crusty with blood, bright with pain. Closing his eyes, he stretched in the cool sheets and derived a wicked pleasure from the contrast.

He heard the clink of plates on the countertop, and knew that it was time to haul himself back into the world.

She was still wearing only her t-shirt, her long legs gold and lean in the early light. He came up to her from behind, full-mast, and wrapped her in his arms, pressing himself against her and burying his nose in her hair.

"Good morning, pretty girl," he said.

She paused, smiled, and leaned her head to the side, baring her neck to him, which he dutifully kissed. A splinter of memory flickered into light, his shameful jealousy over Alicia, and he blew it away like ash.

"Good morning," she said. She reached behind herself and wrapped her fingers around his cock through his boxers. "I thought you were going to miss breakfast."

"Madness."

"The eggs are going to burn."

He released her with a show of reluctance. She gave him a final squeeze and abandoned him to rescue the eggs from the range. He shambled to the coffee pot and poured himself a mug. The hours ahead began to unfold in his mind, revealing little responsibilities, little parcels of free time. He began to organize his day.

"Whose phone is that?"

He tensed. Her tone was light, but that didn't mean he wasn't on dangerous ground. "Some chick's," he said. "She left it at the bar."

"So you brought it home?"

"I forgot I had it. There was a fight. She dropped it, and I was distracted."

Carrie scraped eggs onto two plates, lifted bacon still sopping with grease from a frying pan to join them. She sat at the table with him and together they ate in what he imagined was a comfortable silence.

"Was Alicia there with her new boyfriend?" she asked, after a while.

"Yeah. They want to have a double date with us."

"That sounds awful."

"I know. Maybe we could rope in a few more people and have a triple date, or even a mass date."

"Now it sounds like you're talking about murder."

"Right?"

Carrie reached across the table and pulled the phone toward her. Will felt an unaccountable twinge of anxiety. "What are you doing?" he said.

"Trying to find out whose phone it is, dummy. Why, should I not look? Am I going to see something I don't want to see?"

"No. Why would you say that?"

"I don't know."

"I'm not lying about the phone, Carrie."

"I know. I believe you."

But an unidentifiable discomfort had been introduced between them, which neither would directly acknowledge and which unfolded invisibly over the table like a sick bloom. Will got up and took his dish to the trash, where he scooped the remains of his breakfast. If Carrie noticed or cared, she gave no sign. Instead she took this as her cue to access the phone and begin her investigations.

Will was looking at the coffee pot, contemplating the merits of a second cup, when he heard Carrie yelp.

She put the phone on the table and pushed it away from her. "Fuck," she said. And then she grabbed it again. "Who the fuck were you talking to last night?"

"What do you mean? What's going on?"

"You were texting someone on this thing last night." She delivered it like an accusation. He was about to snap a reply when she turned the face of it to him and he saw the last two texts, delivered after he had abandoned the conversation.

The first:

PLEASE

The second, delivered about ten minutes later, was simply a picture. Will squinted at it, couldn't make it out. He took the phone from her and held it closer to his face. A cold wave pulsed from his heart. It was a picture of half a dozen bloody teeth. They were arranged in a cluster on what appeared to be a wooden table; the roots were broken on most of them, as if they'd been wrenched out.

"Jesus Christ," he whispered.

"What the fuck is that?"

He considered it for a moment. He swiped his thumb across the screen and brought it back to the main menu. Weather, App Store, Google, Camera, Messages, Maps. All of it banal. Nothing on here, it seemed, to personalize it. He wondered what he would see if he checked the rest of her messages.

"Don't mess with it, Will. Take it to the cops. Somebody got hurt last night."

"Maybe. Or maybe they're just fucking with me."

She rose without a word and brought her plate to the sink. She kept her back to him as she ran the water over it.

"You know what? It's Wednesday; Derek will be in after his shift. I'll show it to him."

Derek was a cop in the Sixth District. He usually came in with his partner after a shift and spent an hour or two there. He'd saved Will's bacon on more than one occasion: scaring off drug dealers, helping people out the door who didn't want to leave, and just generally making it known that Rosie's was protected. He was a good guy, and Will was happy to have him as a regular. He felt much better about the idea of showing the phone to him than bringing it into the precinct office, where he was pretty sure he'd be laughed out of the building.

Carrie seemed mollified by this. She shut the water off and faced him, leaning against the sink. "What if she comes back to claim it first?"

"I'll just tell her we haven't found it. I'll let the cops deal with it."

She thought about that. "Yeah. Okay. That seems good."

He put the phone back onto the table and pushed it away from him. "So did you get your paper written last night?"

She sighed, as if already exhausted. "Mostly. I have to go over it again before class. Probably rewrite the ending, since I was a zombie by the time I got to it. Then turn it in and hope Steve likes it."

Steve: her English Lit professor. It rankled him that she called him by his first name, but she claimed all the students did. He liked an "informal learning environment." Well, how progressive of him. The fucker. Carrie had been agonizing over a paper on T.S. Eliot's "The Hollow Men" for almost two months, and he was sick of hearing about it. She'd never fretted this much over a paper for any other professor. "I'm sure he'll love it," he said, making no effort to hide the sourness he felt. He knew it was petty, but it felt good anyway.

She cast him a look which he could not interpret. "He better. It's a quarter of my grade."

"Right."

"What about you? What are you going to do?"

"I don't know. I feel like I should check up on Eric."

"Why?"

"He was the one in the fight last night. He got cut up pretty good."

"Well there's a shock. Let him hide under his rock. I'm sure he's fine. People like that always are."

"People like what?"

"The ones who start shit. It's always everyone else who suffers."

"I just want to make sure he's okay. Concern for others is a common human trait. You'll learn that about us in time."

She walked up to where he sat, standing over him and pressing herself close. "Asshole," she said, and kissed him. He felt himself rise to her, and she grinned as she pushed his hands away. "I have to work."

"Evil," he said, pulling her down for another kiss first, then watching as she went to her office in the next room, which was a calamity of stacked papers, earmarked books, discs, DVDs, and zip drives. She settled into her chair in the midst of all of this, as comfortable in the apparent chaos as a fish in its grotto. She clicked the computer on, cradling a mug in both hands while it booted up. Her t-shirt gathered at her waist and Will was briefly mesmerized by the golden cast of her legs in the morning sunlight.

"You're beautiful, you know," he said.

She gave him a sweet smile. "Good boy."

He shambled into the bathroom and started the shower, trying to decide what to do to fill his day until he had to be back at work. There was a lot of empty space until then, and empty spaces suited him just fine.

*   *   *

AS HE WALKED through the dense morning heat, heading toward the bar and Eric's apartment, Steve nested in the middle of Will's mind, bending every other thought toward him like some terrible star. He seemed to represent an inevitable end, and though Will knew himself well enough to understand that this feeling was as much a product of his own insecurity as of anything else, he couldn't escape its pull.

Will had spent his life skimming over the surface of things, impatient with the requirements of engagement. He told himself that this was because he was open to experience in a way most people weren't, that you sapped the potential for spontaneity from life if you regimented your hours with obligation. This rationalization came upon him in college, shortly after he dropped out, converting all that money invested by his parents into so much tinder for the fire.

Most of the time he believed it.

And why not? Women liked him. He was tall, and he stayed fit without too much effort. He was generally cheerful and had an easy charisma. As long as he had a woman in his life and reasonable access to booze and the occasional line of coke, he figured he'd be okay. He'd been working as a bartender since dropping out of school six or seven years ago, and he believed he might just be able to live out the next fifty years of his life in this state of calibrated contentment.

He loved Carrie, he supposed, but love was a tide that came and went. Who knew how long she would stay with him? She was ambitious, and he could tell it annoyed her that he wasn't. He figured her patience would wear out sometime in the next six months. Another reason that being a bartender was such an ideal job. The girls grew like fruits on a tree. You practically just had to reach out and pluck one.

Life so far seemed like a kind of dance to him, and he was pleased to discover that he was pretty good at it. If there was something hollow underneath it all, a well of fear that sometimes seemed to pull everything else into it and leave him clutching the stone rim for fear of falling into himself, well, that was just part of being human, he supposed. That's what the booze was for.

This line of thought brought him back around to Alicia, and her irritating infatuation with her little hipster douchebag beau-du-jour, Jeffrey. Alicia played the field even more shamelessly than he ever had, and while that intimidated him at first, he eventually came around to admiring her for it. She'd sit at the bar by herself and they'd bullshit about work, her latest boyfriend, his newest girlfriend. When Carrie came along and stuck around longer than most, Alicia had the good sense to spare her from attack, without even having to be asked. Will found that impressive. They hadn't ever slept together – a fact which apparently never crossed Alicia's mind, but which lodged like a seed in his brain and had since sprouted a snarl of tangled roots, until it was hard for him to think about anything else whenever she was around.

He'd always figured it was just a matter of time, and he was content to wait until the moment was right – when Carrie was gone, or when they were just drunk enough that it didn't matter. But then Jeffrey happened along, and all of a sudden things were different. He'd known it the first time she pushed back at him when he started wondering aloud if hipsters could only have sex with an ironic attachment, and whether that attachment required batteries.

"Leave him alone," she'd said.

"Who?"

"Don't be an asshole. I know you're talking about Jeffrey. Lay off the kid. He's okay."

"Just okay? Maybe you do need batteries."

"Fuck off, Will."

He'd like to say that was the last time he'd taken a cheap shot at Jeffrey, but it wasn't. Sometimes he just couldn't resist. Alicia started to ignore it, until it wasn't much fun anymore. He contented himself with knowing that Jeffrey couldn't last much longer, that Alicia's appetite and her impatience with ridiculous men would spell his doom at any moment.

But he'd been waiting for a while now, and he suspected Jeffrey's unlikely heroics last night had given him an extended lease.

He pulled out his phone and dialed Alicia.

"Get a beer with me," he said when she answered.

"Fuck, dude, what time is it?"

"Are you still asleep? It's like ten o'clock."

"I didn't get to sleep until sunrise."

Well, that was the last thing he wanted to hear. "So are you going to come get a beer with me?"

"No, asshole, I am not. I'm going back to sleep."

"When did you turn into a pussy?"

"That is so wrong. And so are you. Maybe I'll see you tonight. Have one for me, okay?"

She hung up.

He pocketed the phone again and kept walking, a cold gulf opening in his chest. Nothing he felt made any sense, and he knew that. He knew he was skirting dangerously close to infidelity, was practically inviting it, but he didn't feel the pang of guilt he knew he should. There was just a need, and he had to answer it.

The thought of going in and having a beer without Alicia with him was too depressing to countenance, so he maintained his heading, resigned to checking in on Eric instead.

His apartment was located above the bar, with a metal staircase affixed to the side of the building, terminating in a small balcony and a front door. You could access the place without being noticed from inside the bar, for which he was grateful. Rosie herself worked the morning shift, and if she saw him, she'd call him in and fill his head with her outrageous opinions. Will crept up the stairs and knocked on Eric's door.

Will found himself hoping that he wouldn't answer. He was having a hard time remembering the impulse that drove him here. They'd never been close – hell, they barely qualified as friends – and standing here in the heat of a bright Wednesday morning, Will felt mother-hennish and ridiculous.

But the thunk of a deadbolt retracting into the doorframe scuttled any hope he had of leaving unnoticed. The door swung open into a cool darkness, and Eric was standing there in his underwear, his hair matted with sweat despite the air conditioner Will could hear clattering away somewhere in the depths of the apartment. The right side of Eric's face was a Technicolor nightmare of scabbed and torn flesh. Dried blood speckled his face and shoulders.

"Holy shit, Eric."

Eric spoke without moving his jaw. He was clearly in vast pain. "What is it?"

"I came to check on you. You need to go to the hospital, man. I'm calling an ambulance."

"No."

"Fuck that. Yes." He reached for his pocket.

Eric took his elbow and brought him inside, shutting the door against the heat. "It's not as bad as it looks."

"Dude, you can barely talk."

He made a vague gesture toward his face. "Swollen. That's all. Come inside."

Will followed him into the kitchen, which was cluttered in the typical way of a single guy who partied too much. Take out boxes on the counter, trash overdue for removal, a few plates in the sink. In the living room he could see some clothing piled in a corner. Eric shook some pills out of a bottle on the counter and swallowed them dry. "Buddy of mine can stitch this up."

"A buddy of yours? What is this, Afghanistan?"

"Can't afford a hospital."

He moved slowly into the living room, one hand in front of him as though he were looking for balance, as though he were still drunk. When he made it to the couch, he collapsed onto it and unfurled like a caterpillar. The blinds were drawn on the room's only window, and the apartment had the cool, dank atmosphere of a cave. "Thank your friend for me," he said.

"What friend?"

"Guy who saved my ass last night. The one banging your girl."

Will felt both irritated and irrationally thrilled. "Alicia isn't my girl."

"Okay, man." His voice was starting to drift.

"Who was that guy you were fighting with?"

Eric didn't answer. His breathing calmed, water finding its level.

"Okay. Anyway. I was just checking in. I'll let you sleep."

Eric, eyes still closed, put out a hand. For an awkward moment, Will thought he meant for him to hold it. "Don't leave me," he said, his voice bleary with painkillers and the proximity of sleep. "Nightmares."

Will felt a sudden shame at having witnessed this nakedly weak gesture, this plea in the dark; it was a gross and bewildering intimacy, and he wanted to pretend he hadn't heard it. Reluctantly, though, he found a place to sit down by moving a laundry basket from a chair to the floor. "Okay," he said. "I'll hang out for a little bit."

He waited for Eric to drift off to sleep, watching his face twitch, his eyes spin beneath his eyelids. He was growing cold in the frigid blast of the AC, but Eric was still covered in a thin sheen of sweat. Below them, at Rosie's Bar, someone fed some money into the jukebox and a dull bass throbbed its way up through the floor, ringing the bones in his body. It would drive him mad, that constant, subdermal growl. He watched Eric fade away, and wondered what black dreams slid through his brain.

FEELING AIMLESS AND obscurely unsatisfied, Will walked back home, where he planned to crash on the couch and play video games until Carrie came back from class. He didn't like spending time by himself, for the most part; silence unnerved him, left him feeling unanchored and threatened. The froth of the video games was partially successful in keeping that silence at bay, but after a while it started to chew through his little pixelated boundaries, and he would be forced to find some other manner of distraction.

So it was with relief that he sensed someone else at home, as though a passage through the air had sent ripples brushing his skin as he entered.

"Carrie?" She should still be in class, but she might have come home early. No one answered. He passed through the kitchen, through the living room, and stopped in their bedroom. The place was empty. Feeling mildly foolish, he planted himself in front of the TV and booted up his video game console.

He was an American solider half an hour into a jungle heavily seasoned with hostiles and a good five minutes away from a hotly defended save point when the phone chimed. He paused the game and fished his phone from his pocket.

Blank. No messages.

His blood cooled several degrees when he realized which phone it had been. He set his own down and removed the other one from his pocket, the bright yellow one with the hearts. Its face was lit, the little green text box signifying a message received. He tapped it with his finger. It was from someone named Jason.

Hey bartender.

He looked at it for several seconds before deciding not to answer. He leaned back and unpaused the game. A sniper took a shot at him from the dense foliage. He keyed himself into a crouch.

It buzzed again, and he glanced over.

U want it?

Fuck you, he thought.

Buzz: *Keep it.*

He dropped the controller and typed a response. *Don't want ur goddam phone. Pick it up at the bar tonight.*

A moment passed. *Did u look at all the pretty pictures?*

He typed. *Maybe I should take it to the police._*

Take a look. Might like what u see.

He waited, but nothing else came from the phone. The video game was frozen on the death screen. A blurry image of his avatar's bullet-riddled corpse lay behind the reset prompt.

He switched it off and gave his full attention to the yellow phone. It felt like a conduit of some dark energy, and he felt uncomfortable holding onto it. He placed it on an end-table beside the couch and called up the menu. The camera icon pulled his eye toward it, as though it exerted its own peculiar gravity. He touched the icon and scrolled over to the picture gallery.

There were four saved images and a video file. He stared at them a moment, trying to come to terms with what he was seeing, trying to arrange the world in such a way that would accommodate his own mundane life, the daily maintenance of his ordinary existence, along with what he saw arrayed before him in neat little squares, like snapshots of Hell.

He tapped his finger on the first one so it ballooned to fill the screen.

It looked like a close-up shot of a sleeping man's face. He was middle-aged, balding, with a large, flat nose; his face was soft and rounded, like the features of a stone carving which had been worn smooth by centuries of wind and rain. There was nothing sinister about this picture; it might be an intimate portrait taken by a lover, or a dear friend.

The second was the same man from the same angle, but taken from a few feet further away. In this picture the man was clearly dead, felled by a violent strike to the head. The rounded dome of the man's skull, cropped out of the first picture, was here depicted in its shattered complexity: bone and brain and blood extruding from the crown like a psychedelic volcano caught in mid-expulsion. The man was lying on the sidewalk. The blood around his head reflected a disc of overhead light, a streetlamp or a flashlight. The picture had been taken at night. He noticed what appeared to be a wedding band on the man's left hand, which lay palm up, white and plump.

The third picture revealed a new setting. This one had been taken indoors, under a harsh light, probably a fluorescent. Seventies-style wood paneling covered the wall in the background. A utilitarian white drafting table occupied the foreground, and resting atop it was the same man's head, severed from its body. It sat planted straight on the table;

someone must have taken the time to balance it, to arrange it just so. The wound in his head was not visible from this angle. No blood marred the scene, save the inevitable blackened ring around the neck. It seemed that some care had been taken to clean the blood from his head, primping him like a schoolboy for his yearbook photo. A slender red book lay on the table behind it, partially obscured, its spine facing the camera.

Will tried to slide on to the next one, but his fingers had gone numb and the phone clattered to the floor. He experienced a wild and irrational fear that someone had heard him and would see what he was looking at, and he felt an overwhelming shame – as though he'd been caught looking at the most outrageous pornography, or as though these ghastly photographs depicted his own work.

Putting the phone back on the table, he closed his eyes and forced himself to calm down. His breath was shaky, his nerves jumping. It occurred to him, abruptly, like some divine communication, that he did not have to look any further. He knew something awful had happened, that a murder of grotesque proportions had been committed and documented, and that any further examination was unnecessary. He should go to the police right now and wash his hands of it.

But stopping was unthinkable. He scrolled to the fourth photograph.

In this one, someone had gone to work on the head with an almost medical precision, and an artisan's hand. Using the killing wound as a starting point, the man's scalp had been sliced into a star pattern, and the skin pulled down from the head in bloody banana peels. The soft, generous features of his face, which had suggested to Will only moments ago the close proximity of someone beloved, which suggested both kindness and the passage of time, were obscured now by the bloody undersides of themselves. The skull had been scraped clean, or nearly so. The eye sockets had been scooped hollow. The table beneath the head was festooned with the gory splashes of the artisan's hard labor.

Only the video clip remained. Pressing the button was not like scrolling through the pictures; he could not pretend he was carried by momentum. This was a separate choice. It was his second chance to turn away.

He pressed play.

The video player took a moment to load, and then filled the screen with the shaky image of the head on the table. A blare of static shrieked from the phone as someone said something unintelligible. Will tapped the button to lower the volume, conscious of the sound intruding into the atmosphere of his apartment, like a species of ghost. He checked over his shoulder, the sense of proximity to another person prickling his nerves once more, and then held the phone close to his face to be sure he wouldn't miss anything. Shame, fear, and a weird thrill filled his body.

"Hold it steady. Jesus." A young man's voice.

The view stabilized, holding firm on the severed head, which was canting slightly to one side. The fourth picture had already been taken: careful ribbons of flesh suspended like wilted petals over the dead man's face. The top of the skull had been shaved down, leaving a red, raw hole just above the temple. A girl stepped into frame, her back to the camera. She had straight blond hair, an athletic body. She straightened the head again, held it a moment to make sure it stayed in place.

"Oh my god I can feel it," she said, and jerked her hands away.

"Get the fuck out of the picture!" Another girl's voice.

She retreated, and a calm settled over the image. A slight movement of the camera as a heart pounded hard in the chest. A stifled, nervous giggle. The head shifted slightly, as if it had heard something and had to turn a fraction to listen more closely. Then it moved again, and something seemed to shift in the darkness of its open skull.

"Oh shit." High pitched, genderless.

Four thick, pale fingers extended from inside the hole and hooked over the forehead. Someone screamed off camera and the image skewed wildly. The video ended.

"Will?"

"Fuck!" He flipped the phone over, turning to see Carrie standing beside him. He felt slow and disjointed, as though he'd dropped a tab of acid. "When did you get home?"

"Just now." She wasn't looking at him, though. "What are you looking at?"

"Nothing."

"I thought you were going to turn that in to the police."

"Yeah. Tonight. I said I'd do it tonight. Jesus, what time is it?"

"I came home early. Skipped math. What are you looking at, Will?"

"I said nothing. Just…" He stood up and put his arms around her in a belated welcome. There was nothing genuine about the gesture, and she pushed him away, plainly irritated.

"Give it to me."

He just shook his head, looking at the ground between them. He could not let her see what he'd just seen. "No. Carrie, just trust me. You don't want to."

He felt her staring at him. "Is that Alicia's phone?"

"What? No! What does that even mean?"

"You know what the fuck it means."

"I can't believe this. I can't believe you're still hung up on this. My friends can only be guys? Really? What about Steve?"

This didn't get the rise out of her he was hoping for. She looked at him calmly and said, "What *about* Steve?"

"He's into you. He wants to fuck you."

"So what? I'm not fucking him."

"But you want to."

"No. I don't. You want to check my phone? See if I have any pictures of him on it? You want to see if I've sent him pictures of my tits? Go check it. It's in my purse in the kitchen. Go."

He shook his head, but the temptation was real. Was she bluffing? Did she know that he wouldn't do it? What if he surprised her and really looked? What would he find? "No," he said. "I trust you. I wish you trusted me too."

"I want to trust you. But you're fucking looking at *something* on some cunt's phone and you're acting guilty as shit!"

Of course, she was right. Nothing about his behavior signaled anything good. He knew that. He retrieved the phone from the table and placed it into her hand. "You don't want to see," he said. "You really don't. It's awful."

"What is it?"

He thought about the fingers. "I don't know."

She sat down, and she opened the files.

He watched it all a second time with her. When she was done, she returned it to him, her hand shaking. He stared at her face the way he would a television screen, waiting for something to happen on it, waiting for it to give him something to react to.

"Is that Garrett? The one who was texting last night?"

That thought hadn't even occurred to him. "I don't think so. These were taken earlier. They were already on the phone."

"Call him."

"What? No."

"Then give it to me. I'll do it."

He clutched the phone more tightly. He felt as though they were debating opening the cage of a starving tiger. "Why, Carrie? It's a bad idea."

"I want to know if he's still alive. I don't want to think about someone dying like that while you ignored him."

"Ignored him?"

"He was asking for help! He was begging you!"

"Oh, fuck that," he said, a surge of guilt turning quickly to anger. "No one's dead, for God's sake." He activated the screen and went back to Garrett's last written text.

PLEASE

He summoned Garrett's number and called it.

Carrie stared at him as he waited for an answer, the phone trilling lightly into his ear. After a moment it stopped ringing. He brought the phone away from his ear a fraction of an inch, thinking at first that it had been disconnected, but something about the quality of the silence told him otherwise.

"Hello?"

Something was alive in that silence.

"Garrett? Hello?"

It spoke. It sounded broken and wet, like something sliding itself together in a slurry of blood and bones. A tongue testing the border of language. Liquid syllables collided and slipped past each other. It sounded too close, like it was already living in his head.

He threw the phone across the room in a reflex of disgust, Carrie's barked cry of shock lost in the echo of the voice leaking from his ear like a thread of blood. The phone came apart in two pieces, and Carrie was already racing toward it, leaving him to rub at his ear with the heel of his hand, tears he didn't even know he was crying trailing down his cheek.

Carrie crouched on the floor, fitting the battery back into the phone, snapping its shell back into place. "Was that him? Was that Garrett?" She sounded panicked.

And why would that be, he wondered, the fear and the disgust of a moment ago settling into a thick soup of anger. She didn't have to listen to that voice.

"No," he said. "It was nobody. Nobody was there."

WEDNESDAYS WERE ALWAYS among the slowest nights of the week, so there was plenty of time for the fear to grind away at the levees he'd built to keep the mounting panic at bay. He felt it threaten to breach every time the door swung open, and he hated himself for it. He didn't know if he'd be able to recognize any of them again, even if they did show up. All college kids looked to him as if they came from the same homogenous gene pool, as if they were all grown in some remote basement laboratory. Arrogant, loud, their little faces as yet unmarked by the heart's weather – they were like bright, wriggling grubs. Members of the Larval Class.

He drank a little more than normal that night, riding his usual buzz a little further into the red. The clientele was sparse enough and familiar enough, though, that he could afford to work with dulled senses.

Derek, the cop, did eventually show up, his partner in tow. They fetched their beers from him and settled into their customary orbit around the pool table, the rails of normal activity so comfortable and rigid that it seemed nothing peculiar could possibly exist in the world.

He and Carrie did not discuss what they had seen on the phone. She'd looked at the pictures, watched the clip, while he peered over her shoulder. She was quiet the whole time, until the fingers crept over the rim of shaved bone, and she uttered a high, small sound. Then they watched it several more times. Somewhere in there, she cried. Then she stopped. When it was time for him to go, they didn't say anything to each other, or kiss each other. Something dead was in the air with them, its limp black wings pressing them flat.

He didn't consider giving the phone to Derek. His mind corrected for its presence, setting up new neural links to avoid its consideration altogether, so that it existed like a black hole in his brain.

At some point, Alicia came in without Jeffrey. He felt an immediate lightening of his spirit, and her arrival seemed like a kind of justice to him, as though this were some secret communication from the universe, some kind gesture to balance the scales for him. She took her usual stool and he mixed her usual drink. The comfortable click of the pool balls punctuated the low chatter of Derek and his partner, Sam Cooke crooned easily from the jukebox, and it was as though the true order of the world had nestled back into place.

"Quiet in here tonight," Alicia said. "You hear anything about Eric?"

He'd actually managed to forget about Eric. "Yeah, actually. Went to see him this morning. He's cut pretty good, but he won't go to the hospital. He thinks he's Rambo."

"You tell Derek about it?"

"Not yet. I'm sure it'll come up." He didn't want to talk about Eric. "So where's Jeffrey tonight?"

Alicia looked irritated and her gaze travelled along the rows of bottles behind him. "He's being an asshole. I'm punishing him."

"Really? What did he do?"

"Like I said. Being an asshole. Anybody come in to claim that phone?" The mention of it loosed a dark tide through his brain, and he found himself reaching for the Jameson. "Not yet." He poured them both a shot.

"Just this one," Alicia said. "I have to go easy tonight."

"Why?"

"I just don't feel like being wasted. I want to try to cut back."

He wondered if that meant he'd be seeing less of her. The thought was terrifying in a way that even the strange video was not. A great sorrow, disproportionate and bewildering, moved through him. "You don't have to get wasted," he said, trying to sound normal. "Just do what I do. Maintain the buzz. It's like surfing."

"You don't have to tell me how to drink, Will."

They drank the shots; and then, as is the way of these things, they drank a few more. The night achieved its rhythm. Derek and his partner shot a few more games, then ambled outside into the course of their own lives. As they left, Will did not spare a thought for the phone he failed to tell them about. The dull anxiety he felt each time the door opened to admit someone new did not abate completely, but as midnight swung around and receded, it faded to a quiet hum. The whole event retracted into a dim kernel of absurdity. Alicia stayed the whole shift, easygoing and flirtatious, just like the old days. She laughed at his dumb jokes, made a few of her own. He felt like a human being again.

When Doug came in to relieve him at two, he snagged a half-full bottle of bourbon from the shelf and swung it like a pendulum in front of Alicia. "I don't want to go home yet," he said.

"Me neither."

"Let's go up to the levee and kill this thing."

Her eyes unfocused for a moment, and he could actually see the doubt pass over her face. It stung.

"Come on, woman."

"Okay. Let's go."

Once they were in his car and on the road, he said, "Listen to this, it's beautiful," and keyed in a Pines song called "All the While," a sweet, quiet rumination which filled the precarious space between them with warmth, a place for them to exist in soft and bleary community. The lights outside washed across the windshield, casting a glow onto her skin and then painting it with darkness again. She rested her forehead against the window and said, "You know what I like about you, Will? When you say something is beautiful, it really is. That word means something to you." He absorbed the compliment. It filled him up.

He parked in the grass and together they ascended the levee's steep gradient, where a walking path snaked across the top. They crossed it and walked a little beyond, settling into the grass along the downward slope. The Mississippi was huge and silent at their outstretched feet, moving the earth's dark energy through the night. The air was humid and close; clouds cruised across the stars above them. Their shoulders were pressed together as they lay back and watched them. Will took a pull from the bottle and passed it to her; she did the same.

"This is nice," he said.

"Yeah. No people. I like no people."

"Me, too."

She angled her head so that it rested on his shoulder, her eyes closed sleepily. He turned to her, his nose in her hair. "You smell good," he said.

She smiled. "Mmm."

"You ever wonder how things could have been?"

She took a moment to answer, but only a small one. "Yes," she said.

He kissed her forehead. Her breath stilled. He did it again, and this time she turned her face up to him, her eyes still closed, and offered her lips. He kissed her there with disbelief that such a thing might be happening to him, with a sense of a great engine beginning at last to turn, with a cresting joy. They kissed tentatively, their lips only grazing, and then more deeply, until they turned their bodies to each other and he put a hand on her cheek. He grazed his fingers across her ear, down the side of her face, and then down to her breast. He felt her bra underneath her shirt, wanted to pull it aside, touch skin to skin. He felt her fingers dig into his hair and his back.

And then she pulled away, pressing her hand against his chest. "Stop, Will."

"But…"

"Stop. Please. I'm sorry. I'm really sorry."

He sat up, dismayed. "Why? What's wrong?"

"You know what's wrong." She sat up too, adjusting her shirt, brushing her hair back behind her ears. There was more space between them now.

"Is it Jeffrey?"

"Of course it's Jeffrey. And it's Carrie, too. Come on, Will."

"Why? Why *him*, for Christ's sake? I don't understand it."

She shook her head. Her face was flushed, and her lower lip trembled. "I don't know. I'm sorry. I'm horrible."

He put his hand on her back. "No, Alicia."

Arching away from his touch, she said, "Don't."

He sat there, feeling ridiculous, feeling like something essential had been blasted away from inside him. "I'm sorry."

"Let's just go back."

They walked back to the car, and when he started the engine, she reached down and switched off the music. They drove back to the bar in a painful silence. He pulled in behind the place she parked, his headlights illuminating the license plate, the rear window. He saw the empty seats in there and imagined them both sitting inside, in a kinder universe, adjacent to this one, where that would be a normal thing, where they both belonged in the same place. He said, "She doesn't love me, you know."

She looked at him with genuine sorrow. "I'm sorry for that. If that's true, then I really am."

"Does he love you?"

She nodded. "I think he really does," she said.

"I do too, you know."

"I know you do." She put her hand on his cheek, and the gentleness of it nearly made him cry. "I'll see you tomorrow night, okay?"

"Yeah. Okay." He could feel the tears in his eyes, knew that she could see them. He didn't care.

She kissed him quickly, chastely. "You're a good man, Will. Maybe the best one. Good night."

"Good night," he said.

He was anything but a good man. He knew it. He watched her pull away from the curb and disappear around the corner. Then he rested his head on the steering wheel and sat there for a while.

BY THE TIME he arrived back home, the sun was bruising the sky in the east. He pulled in behind Carrie's car on the side of the road, shut the engine off, and leaned back in his seat with his eyes closed. Something big was trapped inside him, some great sadness, and he felt if he could cry, or even articulate it in speech, it would relieve the pressure and provide him some measure of relief. But he couldn't reach it. He couldn't find a way to address it. He wondered if it would become the thing that defined him. He imagined himself in the third person, as someone observed and understood by an invisible witness. Would there be room for sympathy? Or would he be damned by it?

The car was a liminal zone; as long as he stayed there he would not have to face either Carrie or Alicia again. It seemed an attractive prospect. He could easily go to sleep here, let the heat of daylight wake him up in an hour or two. He could think of something to tell Carrie.

He was pretty sure he could think of something.

His phone chimed in his pocket, and he fumbled it hurriedly out, thinking for one incandescent moment that it might be Alicia.

It was Carrie. The disappointment was almost physical. He looked at their apartment across the street. The porch light was on, but everything inside seemed dark. That didn't really mean anything, though.

He accepted the call and said, "Hey. Sorry I'm so late. I'm right outside. I'm on my way in."

The call disconnected.

A familiar cold tide flowed through his chest. He told himself she was just angry with him, that she had a right to be – more than she knew –

and she'd simply hung up on him. That he would go inside and take what he had coming. But he knew it was something else. When the phone chimed a text received, he found himself unable to make himself look. He stared at the icon for a long time, feeling that strange, unreleasable presence swell inside of him. Finally, he slid his thumb across the screen and looked at the text.

It was another picture. Taken from inside his house, the lights off. The perspective was from the kitchen, directed at the door to Carrie's study, but angled in such a way that the picture did not afford a look into it. Only the cool blue glow of an active computer screen, radiating from inside her study like a heat signature, gave any hint of a human presence.

Will crossed the street, feeling powerfully dislocated from the world. The door was still locked. He applied his key to it and it swung silently open, spilling the darkness of the interior over him. The air was warm. He stepped inside, attuned to each convulsion of his heart. He knew he should find a weapon, but the actual doing of it seemed too complicated. Easier to just walk into the black cave of his home and accept what waited there.

"Carrie?"

He entered the kitchen. He stood precisely in the spot the photo had been taken. There, bleeding from her study, was the blue glow of the computer screen.

"Carrie? Are you awake?"

He got no answer.

He stepped up to the door and peered in.

She was sitting in her chair, elbows on the desk, leaning in close to the screen. Her right hand was on the mouse, still as a held breath. Something was moving on the screen.

"Carrie. Are you okay?"

"Huh?" She looked at him, blinking at the adjustment. "Oh. Hey. Sorry, I didn't know you were home. What time is it?"

"It's past five, honey." He looked at the screen. She was watching a video of a black tunnel. The walls glistened with moisture. The camera moved through it slowly and smoothly, as if it were gliding along a track.

"Oh man. Really? I lost track of time." She rubbed her eyes.

"What's that? Are you researching something?"

She switched off the screen. "No. That's something else." She arose from her chair and draped her arms around his shoulder. "Are you just getting home?"

"Yeah. I stayed after the shift. Played a few games of pool. Just hung out."

"Good. I like you to have fun." She kissed him sleepily. "Let's go to bed."

"Did you send me a picture a few minutes ago? Did you try to call me?"

She frowned, put her forehead on his shoulder. "No. Maybe? I don't think so. I can't really remember. I feel foggy."

"Are you drunk?"

"I'm just really tired, Will. Come on. Let's go to bed." She headed in that direction, attempting to drag him along behind her.

"I'll be right there, okay?"

She continued on by herself, walking like someone drugged, sagging from her own bones.

He checked the apartment thoroughly. In closets, under the bed, in the pantry. The place was empty. After double-checking the lock on the front door, he followed her to bed. He stared at the ceiling until the rising sun painted it with light, Carrie still snoring beside him. Only then did he manage to close his eyes and lose himself from the world.

THEY BOTH SLEPT into the early afternoon. They awoke groggy and irritable. A heavy weight swung in Will's skull, moving at a slight lag to the rest of him. He moved ponderously into the bathroom, where he took a scorching shower. He felt unaccountably filthy, as though he'd been steeped in sewage. The soap and hot water did nothing to change it. He considered, briefly, that he was feeling guilt about his encounter with Alicia, but in fact the only thing he felt about that was a horror at her rejection.

In the living room, Carrie was sitting on the couch, staring at the window, her hands folded together on her lap. The blinds were still drawn, and the day was a pale white blur beyond them. She noticed him come in, and gave him a wan smile. He had a hard time returning it, but he did.

"What do you think it is?" she said.

"What do you mean?"

She opened her hands, and the yellow phone was there. "The pictures. The video." Her face looked wrong. Maybe she was sick.

"I don't know."

"I thought you were going to give this to Derek."

He shrugged. He resented the question; it felt invasive. "I didn't want to."

"Why not?"

"I don't know. Just – don't worry about it. I will tonight."

She didn't respond. Instead she activated the phone and opened the picture album.

"What are you doing?"

"I'm looking at them," she said simply.

He joined her on the couch and leaned into her, looking as well. "I don't think this is a good idea," he said. She scrolled to the pictures of the severed head, pausing on the first one.

"I Googled that guy's name last night. Garrett? Checked if there were any references on nola.com to someone with that name who went missing or was hurt. I didn't find anything."

"We don't know that anything happened to him," Will said.

She ignored this bit of absurdity. "Then I Googled other words."

He felt queasy. "Like what?"

"I don't remember. A bunch of stuff. Voices on the phone, trading images of violence, death cults, that sort of thing."

He shook his head, unable to process what he was hearing. "Death cults?"

"Well I don't know, Will! What the fuck are these people doing? Texting each other these things?"

"Carrie, did you go *looking* for it?"

"I was trying to figure this out!"

He stood and started pacing, his body sparking with an energy as much excitement as fear. "Well? Did you find anything?"

"I can't remember," she said quietly. He thought of the dark, wet tunnel on the screen last night.

"Don't go looking again," he said.

Carrie sighed, putting her forehead in her hand. The phone lay limply in her other one. "Don't tell me what to do, Will."

He put out his hand. "Give it to me."

"Excuse me?"

"Please. Please, Carrie. Give it to me. I'm going to give it to the police, like I should have done last night."

"No you won't." She set it on the end table, and left him to fetch it himself. "People look so normal on the outside," she said.

"What are you talking about?"

"Inside it's all just worms."

He strode toward the end table and snatched up the phone before she could change her mind. "I don't understand you," he said.

She arose from the couch and disappeared into the bedroom, emerging a while later dressed for the day.

"Have a good night at work," she said.

"Just like that?"

"Give up the phone tonight. Then we'll talk." With that, she was gone.

He fell onto the couch, wanting to be angry. She had no right to give him an ultimatum. He's the one who found the damn thing, he's the one who saw the pictures and tried to protect her from them, he's the one who'd had to listen to that awful voice after she insisted he make the call. The more he thought about it all, the more righteous he felt.

But he still couldn't get angry.

He wasn't sure what he was supposed to feel. The spikes of fear he'd experienced earlier always seemed to retreat to a low-grade anxiety during the day. He couldn't bring himself to believe in what he was seeing. This had to be some kind of elaborate joke, or maybe one of those bizarre role-playing games, and he'd been caught up in it. If anything, he was less inclined to turn the phone over to the police for fear of being laughed at.

He took the opportunity to check her computer in the office room, personal space be damned. He booted it up and toggled her history. Some .edu sites, links to papers on T.S. Eliot, a few celebrity gossip sites, a lengthy spell of window shopping at Amazon. Somewhere in that time the weight of what she'd seen shifted her focus; what started as a perusal of furniture and clothing ending with a browse through the true crime section, followed by books on the occult. There were links to a few sites after that, but not many – ancient, horribly designed sites about Satanism and witchcraft, hosted on long-defunct platforms with rudimentary interfaces. It was as though she'd been engaging in a geological dig through the strata of the internet's past. From there she seemed to have spent considerable time looking into something called *The Second Translation of Wounds*. The last recorded site visit was time-stamped 11:17. Several hours before he arrived home.

After that, there was no record of her activity. It was as though she'd shut the computer off. Or – he thought, despite his efforts at rationalization – cracked through the lowest stratum to something else.

What had she been looking at?

What did she find?

He shut the computer down. The whole thing made him feel sick. He went into the kitchen and made himself a screwdriver. Two or three more of those and he'd be able to push the whole thing out of his mind.

THE NIGHT WAS surprisingly busy, and at first he was able to lose himself in the tide of work. Most of what he termed the Rosie's Regulars made an appearance: Old Willard, the raisin-faced ex-POW from the Korean War, smiling through his sublimated rage and throwing nasty remarks at tough guys fifty years his junior; Naked Mary, the two hundred and thirty pound exhibitionist who was good for two or three appearances a month and always concluded her stay with a pool game played in the nude; Scotty, the oyster-shucker from down in the Quarter who sang Frank Sinatra tunes at the top of his lungs, even though he'd been living under the aegis of the Jim Crow laws when most of those songs had been popular; along with the ordinary flotsam of an ordinary night, a number of which Will counted among his friends – at least as far as a word like that stretched when they only came to see you for the booze.

Even the roaches were at a low ebb, as the bar had been visited by an exterminator earlier in the day. He found nearly a dozen of them on their backs, their legs moving lethargically, as though they'd been caught sweetly dreaming.

But for the absence of Alicia, it was shaping up to be a banner night at Rosie's.

Derek and his partner showed up too, drifting to their usual haunt at the pool table. Will felt the weight of the yellow phone in his pocket. He tried to make eye contact with Derek, but his attention was focused elsewhere. Later, then. The phone wasn't going anywhere.

Around ten-thirty, a sourness began to set in. Alicia's continued absence started to feel like an indictment. The bar was full, the jukebox was rattling on its feet, the vibe was good, but the joy he'd been taking in the work seeped away, and his mind disengaged. She was blowing him off. He remembered their kiss with a beautiful, unkind clarity. He needed her to be here so he could apologize to her, so he could be reassured by her, and so he could impress upon her with nothing more than the force of his absolute conviction that the love he bore her was the purest thing he had ever felt.

Perhaps it was because of this distraction that he did not immediately recognize the clean-cut kid leaning across the bar at him, his arms folded beneath him and an ugly half-grin climbing up one side of his perfect face. He looked at the kid, waiting for him to place his order, some pugilistic impulse refusing to utter the first syllable in the exchange. If the kid was too cool to speak, he could fucking go without.

And then he recognized him. His face must have betrayed him, because the kid gave him the full-wattage smile, the one that charmed the girls right out of their clothes, like snakes from their baskets. "Took you a minute," he said.

Will looked behind him for the other kids, the ones too young to come up and order for themselves. The bar was crowded, but he didn't see them. The table in the corner, where they'd roosted last time, was empty.

"What can I do for you," Will said, trying to play down his momentary shock. Act like he was any normal customer.

"Well, I'm not going to stay long – I forgot my ID." He patted his pockets with a sad smile. "I just wanted to let you know we left you a little present."

The world blurred for a moment. He thought of Carrie, alone at home, staring into her computer screen. "Leave her alone," he said. He sounded weak; like a scared little kid.

The other guy smiled and shook his head. "Your girlfriend? Nice tits, butch haircut? No, dude, I'm not talking about her. Hey, you got a thing for dykes or something?"

Will couldn't believe he was saying this to him. In his bar, of all places. Surrounded by his friends. The absolute arrogance of the move was enough to render him breathless. He had a vague sense of people waiting for his attention down the bar. They could keep waiting. "You need to get the fuck out of here right now," he said, "before something bad happens to you."

He realized that this was the best chance he'd have to turn the phone over to Derek. Everybody was right here. He could settle it all right now. But the thought of surrendering the phone made him feel ill. A distant alarm sounded from some deep chamber in his brain as he realized this, but he buried it and focused on the moment.

The kid held up his hands in mock surrender. "No problem, man, no problem."

"Who are you people, anyway?"

He seemed to consider this a moment, and then leaned in over the bar, gesturing Will closer. Against his better judgment, he leaned in too.

"The truth?" he said. "We're nothing but a nice suit of clothes, waiting for somebody to put us on."

"What the fuck?"

"Open your present," he said, and turned to push his way through the crowd. In moments, he was gone.

Will sent Carrie a quick text, and she replied that she was fine. So he continued to work, agitated and jumpy. Fortunately, most of the customers were too buzzed by this point to notice.

When Alicia finally strolled in with Jeffrey, well past eleven, Will felt a thrill of relief. It seemed she was borne in by a tide of inevitable movement, that the slow engine of fate was finally beginning to turn. They took their positions at the end of the bar and turned in to each other, deep in conversation. He poured their drinks and set them down; no exchange of words was necessary. They were functions of an algorithm.

He wouldn't try to wedge himself into their conversation. Usually he was welcomed into it, but tonight they barely gave him notice. That was all right. What he had to say to Alicia would take time and her full attention. He could wait.

Derek tapped the bar for his attention. Will grabbed a cold bottle of Miller Lite from the cooler and went to meet him.

"I heard what happened to Eric," he said, taking the beer and turning it up to his mouth, never breaking eye contact. "Why didn't you call us, man?"

"I did. You guys didn't show up for like an hour."

"I don't mean Sixth Precinct, I mean *us*." He pointed to himself and his partner.

It hadn't even occurred to Will to call them specifically. He shrugged. "I don't know. I didn't know that was something I could do."

"This is our turf, man. We protect it."

"I know."

"Dude. Look at me. When was the last time this place was hit by an underage sting? Hm? When's the last time anybody ever followed up on a noise complaint? *We protect this place.* You have my number, right?"

Will looked at dozens of business cards and personal notes tacked to the wall behind the bar phone, interlaced and overlaid like continental plates. "I know it's up here somewhere."

Derek slid him a card with his name and number on it. "Put this in your wallet. Next time, you call me."

"Okay." Will felt both empowered and chastened.

"So is he all right? Who did it?"

He thought about Eric dwelling in darkness above them, solitary as a monk, cherishing his wound like some acolyte in a cult of pain. He considered what his reaction might be if a couple of police officers – even ones he drank with and played pool with sometimes – came into his apartment at Will's direction. It wasn't something he wanted to think about for long.

"He's okay. I checked on him yesterday. He's cut, but I think it's his pride that's hurt, more than anything."

"What about the guy that did it?"

"I've never seen him in here before. I figure that's between them."

Derek raised his eyebrows. "Dude swings a broken bottle and you figure that's just between them?"

"You know what I mean."

"No, I really don't. You see him, use that card. I want to talk to him. See how tough this bitch really is."

"Okay, Derek."

"I'm serious."

"I know. I will."

Mollified, Derek returned to the pool table, placed some quarters on the edge, and watched his partner finish his game. Will gathered a few dirty mugs from the bar and brought them to the sink. He caught a glimpse of Alicia and Jeffrey from the corner of his eye, and stopped what he was doing.

Jeffrey was staring at him with an expression Will found difficult to interpret. Alicia slouched beside him in an attitude of defeat, her head lowered, her hand cupped over her eyes.

Well, here we go, he thought, and he walked over to them.

"Need another beer, Jeffrey?"

Jeffrey looked at his bottle, which was still half full, and tipped it over with one finger. The contents splashed over the bar top, and the bottle rolled and fell over Will's side, where it landed with a glassy crunch. "Yeah," he said. "That one's empty."

Alicia lifted her head. "Please don't."

Will leaned over until he caught Jeffrey's gaze, and held it. "Are you okay, Jeffrey?" His tone of voice made it more of a challenge than a question.

Jeffrey was not okay. In fact he was grandly drunk, his eyes bloodshot and the skin hanging loosely from his face, like wet laundry. He gave Will a big grin, about as genuine as an alligator's, and clasped his hand. "Hey Will, I'm good, I'm really good. How the fuck are *you*, Will?" His words stumbled against each other.

Will extracted his hand. "You're wasted, man. You should go on home." He looked at Alicia. "You guys started before you got here, didn't you?"

She didn't answer, just watched him with a darkness in her gaze. It unsettled him; he didn't know how to read it. She was probably wasted too.

"Bring me another beer, Will," said Jeffrey.

"I think you're about done for the night, man."

"Bring me another beer, Will."

"Don't take this approach with me, Jeffrey." He looked at Alicia. "Maybe you should get him out of here."

She nodded vaguely. She looked devastated. Obviously, she'd told him. That's what he'd wanted, of course, but somehow he'd imagined it would be different. That she would not be so upset herself. Of course, Alicia was kind, and she would be distraught over the pain she was causing Jeffrey. It would run its course. He tried to catch her eye, to communicate through a glance his own understanding, but she was too involved in getting Jeffrey to his feet to notice.

Jeffrey did not resist too much. He let himself be guided off the stool, but some residual instinct of self-respect wouldn't allow a clean retreat: as she walked him away from where they were sitting, he flicked her half-empty bottle off the bar too. It shattered on the floor.

People were starting to look.

Alicia pulled him harder. "Jeffrey!"

"Bring me another beer, Will," he said.

"You're not a tough guy, Jeffrey," said Will. "Stop acting like one."

They were almost at the door by this time, drawing the curious gaze of the rest of the bar behind them like a net caught in their wake. It was too easy. Will was struck by a perverse impulse.

"Alicia," he said. "I'll call you later."

Jeffrey turned, wrenching his arm free of Alicia's grasp, and walked back toward the bar. Rage clouded his face. Will was fascinated; what was he going to do, vault over the bar? The presence of violence was in the room again, filling it like a gas. He felt ghostlike: a witness to his own life. Something fundamental was about to tip, and he waited for it with a hunger which was curiously distinct from any sense of self-preservation. What he wanted was an irrevocable action, the crossing of a bloody border.

Derek intervened. He stepped in front of Jeffrey, stopping him in his tracks. "We got a problem here?"

The frustration on Jeffrey's face was almost heartbreaking. You could see his heroic plans evaporating right before his eyes. "I thought we were friends," he said to Will, speaking over Derek's shoulder.

"We are friends," Will said. "Come on, man."

"What's the matter with you, you fucking prick?"

Derek poked him hard in the shoulder. "Don't talk to him. Talk to me."

Derek wanted it too; you could see it radiate from him like a stuttering light.

"I don't want to talk to you," Jeffrey said. He didn't sound confrontational; he just sounded sad. All the bravado he'd felt after breaking up the fight the other night, the masculine dream he'd allowed himself to indulge in, was gone. He just stood there, ashamed and ineffectual, tears gathering in his eyes. Alicia took his arm again, shooting a dark look at Will, and led him away. This time, he didn't resist. They pushed through the door, into the world outside.

"Was he crying?" somebody said, and there was a snicker. Then, as if a switch had been flipped, people returned to their own little endeavors. The noise rose, the pool balls clicked, and people approached the bar with money in hand. The night's slow engine began to turn once again.

Derek and his partner finished their pool game and left, waving amiably on their way out the door.

Will felt cheated, somehow. That old hollowness reasserted itself, and he felt a vertiginous pull, as though he stood on its crumbling edge. The image Carrie had been looking at the night before came back to him: the wet, black tunnel, and the silent, gliding passage through it to an unfathomable end.

Something waited down there.

He pulled his phone out of his pocket, ready to dial her.

There was already a message waiting for him. A text from Carrie. Two of them. He quickly slid it open.

I think something is in here with me.

The next was a picture: their own apartment. Their own bedroom. The lights off. A man sitting on the edge of their bed, facing the camera. His arms rested loosely between his legs, and he was buried in shadow. His face seemed somehow misshapen. Will felt his gut clench, felt adrenaline spike in his body. He was breathing hard. His hands shook. He tapped the picture to bring it to the fore, and enlarged it. Squinted at it.

We left you a little present.

A wave of nausea passed over him, and he felt something hot crowd the back of his throat. He stepped out from behind the bar without really thinking about what he was doing. He pushed his way through the crowd. His chest was too tight, he could barely breathe. Somebody called out to him.

"Watch the bar!" he said back. He didn't care who.

In seconds, he was in his car and speeding through the narrow streets, slamming through potholes and across cracked pavement bucked up over the roots of oaks, gunning through intersections. Aware of his recklessness even in the heat of his own panic, he had the stray thought that some kindly angel must be watching over him, shepherding him safely home.

THE APARTMENT WAS quiet, the windows dark. Carrie's car was still parked out front. He didn't know how long she'd been home. Wishing for a gun for the first time in his life, Will sprinted across the street and crept quietly to his own front door. He pressed his ear against it, trying to siphon out the sound of the occasional passing car, the sound of the leaves rustling in a light wind. He was pretty sure it was quiet inside. He tested the knob to see if the door was locked. It was.

So much for sneaking up on the intruder.

Twisting his key in the lock, he grit his teeth at the hard thunk of the bolt sliding back. He pushed the door open while remaining outside.

The lights were out. Nobody came to answer his presence.

"Carrie?"

Still nothing.

"Is anybody in here? Come on out."

By this time, anger had occluded the fear. Someone had come into his house. With Carrie here. The words of that college kid tolled in his skull like funeral bell.

He strode in quickly, flipping on the lights. Two roaches scurried across the floor to hide in a deep crevice between the wall and the floorboards. "Carrie! Are you in here?"

Passing through the kitchen, he yanked open the cutlery drawer so forcefully that it hung from its runners like something disemboweled, spilling half of its contents onto the floor in a bright clatter. He retrieved a chef's knife from the pile, clutched it hard, and kept walking.

The familiar computer screen bleed of light seeped from Carrie's study. He strode to the entrance and there she was, as he'd found her last night, staring into the screen. She seemed unhurt: no blood, no signs of distress of any kind. Her hair was loose and unwashed, and she was dressed for bed. Something in the room stank.

"Carrie. Jesus Christ. Why didn't you answer?"

She did not seem to register his presence.

"Carrie?"

On the screen was the same image: the camera, still moving through the dark, wet hole. This time she'd turned the sound on: a distant, hollow wind, like putting your ear to a seashell. The fear settled back over him with a fluttering silence, birds settling onto a tree. He put his hand on her forehead: she was clammy and sweaty. He realized with a twist of despair that the stink was coming from her: she had pissed herself, and even now sat in a puddle of it.

"Oh fuck."

Facing her, turned away from the rest of the apartment, he felt as though he was standing with his back to the mouth of a bear cave.

Turning around, he said, "Who's here, baby? Is anybody else here?"

He left her sitting there, crept into the kitchen and turned right into the living room. Enough ambient light leaked in through the windows that, after standing there for a moment, he could be reasonably sure it was empty. But the door to the bedroom loomed beyond it, and no light intruded there.

Will clicked on a lamp in the living room. Shadows leaped and scattered, settling immediately into a picture of order and familiarity. The couch, the TV, the framed film stills Carrie prized so much. Light wedged into the bedroom.

"If anybody's in there, you need to come out right now. I swear to God, man. This is no joke."

When no one stepped forth, Will crossed the bedroom's threshold, peering in. The bed was unmade and the sheets were rumpled, which was typical. Neither of them had ever gotten into the habit of making it. A small pile of dirty laundry coiled in one corner of the room, spilling from a full basket. A comic book lay on the floor near his side of the bed, stacked notebooks and textbooks on hers. Nothing appeared out of the ordinary.

He flicked on the light switch, then knelt down and peered under the bed.

The apartment was empty.

Will sat on the bed, the tension unspooling from him in a long, shaky exhalation. He thought of Carrie sitting there still, in a puddle of her own urine, staring at that stupid loop on her computer. He thought of her sending him these pictures. Maybe she was losing her mind. He thought he recalled her mentioning that one of her grandmothers had suffered from some kind of mental breakdown, living out a lonely end in a mental institution. Maybe that kind of thing ran in the family. He didn't know.

A terrible, gaping sadness opened in him, and he put his thumb and forefinger to his eyes to stifle the sudden tears.

The title of the book she'd been looking for floated across his thoughts, unbidden and unwelcome: *The Second Translation of Wounds.*

His phone chimed in his pocket, startling him so badly he jumped.

Garrett's name was on the screen.

"Hello?"

That voice seeped out again: a shard of bone pushed through a throat. A welling of blood. Was it Garrett himself? The thing that had ripped out his teeth? Or something that had crawled out of him? Will listened with tears spilling from his eyes.

CARRIE COULD NOT be coaxed from her chair until he shut her computer down, eliciting from her a small sound of loss. Her eyes, bloodshot and dry, finally closed. She sagged into him, utterly exhausted, and he held her head to his shoulder, wrestling to maintain his own outward calm. Inside, it felt as though pieces of himself were sliding away, like an iceberg calving into the sea. He was hunched behind a panic wall; just beyond it, he knew, must be a correct response. Something simple and easy. But there was also a howling chaos there, a black tumble of fear, and he couldn't face that just yet. He knew, in a distant way, that he was in shock, but he didn't know how to find his way out of it.

The first order of business was to restore sanity to his own home.

He lifted Carrie from her chair, heedless of the urine, and carried her calmly to the bedroom. She did not protest; he thought she had fallen asleep, until he glanced down and saw her eyes were open and unfixed. He laid her on the bed, next to where he'd left his cell phone. He knocked it to the floor with an angry flick of the wrist, as though it were a cockroach that had crawled into their sheets. He ran hot water into the bath, and in moments he had her undressed and submerged to her shoulders. He talked to her while he bathed her, saying nothing in particular – just maintaining what he hoped was a steady, calming flow of speech.

Once the water began to cool, he drained it and guided her out of the bathroom. She seemed to have recovered something of herself. She unhooked her robe from the door and shrugged into it, binding it tightly around her waist. Then she sat on the bed and sighed deeply, still staring at the floor. But she was present this time; she had come back.

Will sat beside her and for a time neither of them said anything. He tried to imagine what might be going through her head, but couldn't do it. His phone, its screen now cracked, blinked at him from the floor. Three missed calls. All from the bar. He didn't even want to imagine what was going on over there. He took it for granted that the job was lost.

"Shouldn't you be at work?" she said, finally.

"Yeah."

"Why did you come home?"

He looked at her. She was still staring at the floor, or at nothing in particular, and he couldn't gauge the weather in her voice. She was no less mysterious for having decided to speak to him. "Do you remember anything that just happened, Carrie?"

Her brow furrowed as she tried to think. "I was looking for something online. Doing some research. Then you called me."

"I didn't call you, Carrie."

"You did. I remember because you were at work and I wondered what it could be about."

"It wasn't me."

"Well your number came up. After that… I don't know. It's hard to think."

The image of the figure sitting on their bed, its head weirdly distorted, floated to the surface of his mind. "Was anybody here tonight?"

This question seemed to require a special degree of concentration. "I think there was." Something in her voice slipped. "Oh my God. I think someone was here."

"Who?"

Carrie shook her head. "I don't know. I was doing research. Your call came in. I remember talking to you."

"Goddamn it, Carrie, it wasn't me!"

She rubbed her finger against her temple – lightly at first, and then with increasing ferocity. Startled, he pulled her hand away. "Am I going crazy?" she said. "Do I have a brain tumor?"

"No, it's… no." He drew in a deep breath. "What's *The Second Translation of Wounds*, Carrie? What were you researching?"

Her face blanched; she leaned over, her head between her knees, and for a moment he thought she was going to puke. But she pulled herself together and sat up again. "It's a book. I was trying to figure out what those pictures were. It was on the table in the video."

The red volume. Of course. "What kind of book is it?"

She shook her head. "I don't know. I can't remember. Something bad. It's something bad. I can't seem to hang onto it."

"What about the tunnel?"

"What tunnel?"

"When I came home… two nights now. You're looking at a tunnel."

"I don't know." Her voice shook. She put her hands on his face and pulled at him, turning his face into a grotesque frown. "What did we see, Will? *What did we see?*"

He didn't say anything. The panic wall stood resolute. No option made sense.

After another moment, Carrie drew in a deep, shuddering breath, and quickly expelled it. "Okay. Well. You have to go back to work. We can't afford you to lose that job."

"Are you serious? I can't go back there tonight."

"At least call them and make sure they didn't loot the place."

"Yeah. Okay." He retrieved his cracked phone from the floor; when he saw there were no new texts or images waiting for him, he felt a giddy relief, and almost laughed. He dialed back the bar. Doug answered; apparently somebody had the good sense to get him in early.

"Will, what the fuck?"

"It was an emergency. I'm sorry. I had no choice. How's the bar?"

"Everything's mostly fine. Are you okay, man?"

"Yeah. I'm good. I'll be back tomorrow night, if I still have a job."

"Relax. We got you covered."

He felt such a tide of gratitude that he had to fight back tears. "Thanks, man."

"Just do what you need to do."

Will started to hang up when Doug started talking again.

"Say that again?"

"I said Eric called down, asking for you. Told him you went home early. I didn't know you guys were buddies."

"We're not. What did he want?"

"He wouldn't tell me. I gave him your number though. It's probably a booty call. I don't judge, brother."

Will barked a laugh. It sounded bad. "Yeah," he said. "Okay."

*   *   *

SOMETIME IN THE dark morning, while Carrie slept, Will crept into her workroom and activated her computer. The image of the tunnel flickered onto the screen, frozen. After a moment, the computer re-connected to the internet, and the image started moving again – drifting through the black tunnel. He glanced up at the URL line; it was blank.

The sound of wind still drifted gently from the speakers. Will was struck with the notion that the screen did not show a descent into the depths, but the perspective of something rising from them. Something dragging itself into the light.

Will reclined in the chair. An unpleasant energy coursed through him, filling him with an urge to action, but what that action might be he didn't know. He went to the freezer and took the bottle of vodka, taking a few good slugs to calm himself.

It worked, at least partly. He was able to sit down again.

He took the yellow phone from his pocket and placed it on the desk. Then he took out his own phone and dialed Alicia's number.

After a long moment, she answered. "Hello?"

"Hey," he said. "It's me."

"Hey, Will. You shouldn't call here."

He leaned closer to the screen, trying to pull an image from the shadows.

"I know. I'm sorry to bother you. I'm just wondering if you're okay."

"I am. Thanks. How are you?"

"Good, I think. So… you told him, I guess."

"Yes. I didn't mean to. Or maybe I did. I don't know."

He thought he could detect something – some scuttling presence – but it could have been just the pixels playing tricks on him.

"It's okay. Is he there with you?"

"Yes. In the other room."

"Is that a good idea?"

"There's nothing to worry about. Everything is fine. Look… I can't talk to you right now. I have to go, okay?"

"Will I see you tomorrow night?"

"I don't know. I have to go. Good night, Will. Don't call back."

He thought he heard another sound riding underneath the hollow wind coming from the speakers. He felt something ripple across his nerves, like a cool breath.

"Yeah. Okay. Good night."

She had already hung up. He put his ear next to the speaker. He strained to hear.

THE NEXT MORNING, Will broke things off with Carrie. He waited until she was fully awake, and they were sharing their usual coffee at the kitchen table. He was abrupt and passionless.

"I think we should break up," he said. "This isn't working."

She did not immediately respond. His instinct was to keep talking, to fill the long silence with all the usual platitudes and excuses, but he stayed quiet.

He told himself he was doing this to protect her. Whatever foulness had wormed into his life was threatening her, and he wanted her well clear of it. He even allowed himself the small fantasy that after it was resolved – however that might be – he would tell her about why he did it, and although they would not be able to repair the hurt he was causing her now, she would at least come to understand his reasons, and to hold him in a higher regard because of them. She would view this as a noble sacrifice.

He told himself, too, that he was just beating her to the punch. That she was going to dump him soon anyway, for Steve the English Professor or for somebody else more accomplished than Will was, and for once he'd like to be on the delivery side of that particular bullet.

But all of that was bullshit, and even he knew it. Though what was happening to them might have catalyzed the action, the real reason was Alicia. He wanted her. He believed, at heart, that she wanted him too. And after last night, he didn't think Jeffrey would be an obstacle anymore.

He waited for the tears and the anger. She sat across from him, her gaze unfixed, almost contemplative. She took another sip from her mug, and he suffered a bad moment in which he thought he hadn't actually said anything at all, that he was still gathering the courage to do it. He felt slippage between himself and the world, like a soundtrack desynchronized from its film.

"Okay," she said.

He nodded dumbly. That wasn't enough. That didn't tell him anything. It didn't tell him what he needed to do next. He gave her a moment to elaborate, but she chose not to take it. So finally he said, "That's it?"

"Yup. That's it."

"Fuck." He leaned back, dismayed and hurt. "Well, fine then. 'Okay.' What a nice capstone."

She looked confused. "Why are you acting offended? You're the one who's breaking up with me."

"Yeah, but do you even care?"

"Not right now I don't. That'll come later. But you don't get to see that."

"I just can't believe how calmly you're taking this." He heard his own voice tremble, start to rise.

"It's been coming for a while. I know you want Alicia. It's too bad she doesn't want you."

"That's not it." He immediately regretted the lie, knowing it would be revealed as such within a matter of days.

"Then what is it? Are you threatened by Steve? Still think he wants to fuck me?"

"No. Come on. Will you stop with that shit?"

"Your words."

"I was being stupid."

"You're still being stupid, Will."

"Well, fuck you." He stared into his coffee, unable to meet her gaze. He felt the heat in his face, knew he was flushed. He tried to settle his breathing. "I'm sorry," he said. "I'm sorry. Will you just let me talk?"

She sat unmoved, watching him with an unearthly calm. "I didn't know I was stopping you. Please. Go ahead."

"It's not Alicia, okay? I wish you would stop with that, because it's bullshit, and it's always been bullshit. It's… it's this stuff with the pictures. The phone. It's dangerous. I don't want you around it."

Finally, he got a reaction. Her face pinched in anger. "Really? You're an action hero now?"

"What? No! Come on, Carrie."

"Can you hear yourself? I'm already 'around it.' It's happening to *me*. You're just a goddamn spectator!"

"That's not fair."

"You're scared. You're a scared little boy. I'm scared too, Will. But I would never have abandoned you to it."

He wanted to cry. This was going as wrongly as it could go. "No, that's not what I mean. Carrie…"

"No, fuck you. I wasn't angry until just now. I was disappointed. I was hurt. But I almost respected you for a minute there, Will. I almost thought you were doing the right thing. But now I'm pissed. So if that's what you wanted, congratulations. You got it."

"It's not what I wanted."

"You don't have any idea what you want. You know what I think you want? Nothing. I think there's nothing there to satisfy. I think you're a mock person, you're some kind of walking shell." She took a breath, and brought her wrist to the corner of her eye to staunch a tear. "I guess you can find a place to crash until you get a new apartment, right?"

For some reason, this hurt worse than anything else she'd said. "Really? Today?"

"What did you expect? That we'd cuddle? Besides, I might be *in danger*, right?"

"Fine." He got up. A terrible weight suspended between his lungs, threatening to upend him. He felt the heat of shame and grief gather in his face. It wasn't supposed to go like this. He made his way to the bedroom and excavated a crumpled duffel bag from the recesses of the closet. He began to shove clothes into it, heedless of what he might actually need. Just random things. When he walked to the bathroom to get his toothbrush and his razor, he heard a stifled sob in the kitchen.

This was the world he'd built. This was his kingdom.

It DIDN'T APPEAR as though anyone had been to Eric's door in the two days since Will had last stopped by. A fly-dappled recycling bin, topped off with beer bottles, had been shoved outside but not carried to the curb, suggesting that at least some effort had been expended in cleaning up inside. Will knocked on the door and waited. When no answer came, he tested the door, and it opened readily for him.

The place stank of sweat and rotting food. Flies buzzed angrily somewhere inside, and a few cockroaches ambled away, incurious and unafraid. Sunlight hacked into the dark interior, and heat spilled out in a thick collapse. The AC that had frozen him the last time he was here had apparently died.

So much for anybody cleaning up. "Christ," he whispered. Then: "Eric? Are you in here?"

He walked down the hallway into the kitchen, which bore evidence of continued neglect. Dishes were strewn around the counter space and piled in the sink, where an odor exuded from a stack of plates like an evil intelligence. Crumbs and stray bits of cereal crunched underfoot. Another handful of roaches perched like lookouts from their pot-handles and their glass rims, their antennae waving in bored appraisal of this new element.

Eric's voice traveled from somewhere deeper in his apartment. It sounded like he was speaking around a mouthful of food.

The living room looked much as it had before, just a little more so: clothes were draped across the back of the stained couch, socks gathered in little colonies in the corners and on the chair. A PlayStation sat in the middle of the floor, long cords extending in black umbilicals to the television, and to the controller resting beside the couch.

There was a different kind of smell in here, something sweeter and fouler. It emanated from the darkened corner toward the back, which led to the bedroom. Will didn't want to go any further; he knew what it was.

But the voice came again, floating out of the bedroom on a current of decay. "Will."

Will stepped into the bedroom. Eric had the blinds drawn, but sunlight leaked in through the slats, giving the room an odd, underwater feeling. Like the rest of the apartment, it was a mess. Eric was lying on the bed in his boxer shorts, the sheets kicked to the floor. He was sheened in sweat. He turned his head to watch Will enter, revealing the hideous wound distorting the left side of his face. It had gotten worse. Crusted with black blood, it had swollen and dried, reopened, dried again. Flies droned around his face, strutted boldly across his skin like little conquistadors. The stink of infection stopped Will at the door.

Eric tried to speak; the wound made it difficult for his mouth to move the way it was meant to. "What do you want?"

"I need a place to crash."

Eric apparently had nothing to say to this. Will couldn't really blame him.

"I need to stay on your couch," he said. "Just for a day or two. Just until Alicia's ready."

Eric shook his head. "No."

"I'm up against a wall, Eric."

"No!" This effort caused him some pain, and he turned his face into the pillow.

Will shook his head. "It's going to be good. I'll even help you clean up a little bit. You'll see." He went back into the living room, ignoring the sounds Eric made. He made a space for himself on the same chair he'd sat in before, while shepherding Eric through his nightmares. He dialed Alicia's number on his phone.

It rang four times before she answered it. "I told you not to call back."

"That was last night! Are you okay? What are you doing?"

"Will – I am trying to fix my life, okay? I need you to stop calling me. It's not helping."

"I left Carrie. I broke up with her this morning."

There was a long pause on the other side. Finally Alicia said, "I'm sorry. I'm sorry to hear that, Will."

"But – that's a good thing. Right?"

"I don't know. That's up to you, I guess."

"But – what? Alicia…"

"Will, I'm with Jeffrey. I love Jeffrey. Do you understand that?"

He shook his head, unable to accept what he was hearing. Unable to accept the magnitude of his mistake. "No, I don't understand it."

"I don't know when we're coming back to the bar. Maybe not for a while, okay? Don't call back. If you really care about me, don't call back."

With that, she hung up.

Will sat back on the couch, waiting for the right feelings to happen. The heartbreak, the anger, the tears. But he didn't feel any of them. What he felt instead was a terrible yearning. He didn't even know what for. But he felt it like a physical ache, like something on fire. He looked at the dark hole of Eric's bedroom, trying to will him into the doorway. They could address their pain with alcohol. Together – as friends. He just needed somebody.

And then, as though he had conjured him with a magic spell, Eric appeared there, leaning against the doorjamb, his flesh gray and loose. "You can't be here," he said. A fresh rivulet of blood had made a path along his jawline, and even now pushed lethargically down his neck.

A thought suddenly occurred to Will. "Eric, did you call the bar last night, looking for me?"

Eric's face clouded over. "No," he said, and turned to go back into his bedroom.

Will leaped from the couch and pinned him to the door frame, putting his face close. The stench of infection shoved its way into his nose, but he ignored it. "It came from here. Who called the bar?"

He was astonished by how weak Eric had become. Just a few days ago he would never have been able to hold him; Eric would have broken his teeth for even trying. But now it was like holding a listless child. "They did. Those freaks."

"What freaks?"

Eric turned his face, exposing the wound. It was spectacular. Will leaned in closer, a grisly curiosity overwhelming his aversion to the smell. It seemed outrageous, something too Hollywood to be real. The edges were swollen and damp with lymph, and they seemed rubbery, like the borders of a mask that could be yanked off. He peered more closely, wondering if he'd be able to see the teeth, the long ridge of the jawbone. As Eric tried to speak, Will could detect the movement of the tongue somewhere in the depths of the injury, like a grub rooting through offal.

"What freaks, Eric? Were they the kids from the bar that night?" Knowing already.

"They said they wanted to give you a present. Now get the fuck off me. I'll kill you. I will kill you." The sustained speech was agony, and Eric's knees buckled. Will caught him underneath his arms and half dragged him back to his bed, where he collapsed limply, finally curling up into the fetal position. He lay there, sobbing like a child, while Will stood over him.

It took him a few minutes before he understood what the present they'd left him was. When he understood, he had to lean his hand against the wall while a tide of vertigo swept through him.

It just needed a place to be born. That's all it ever was.

When the vertigo passed, he knelt beside the bed, placing his hand gingerly on Eric's shoulder.

"Can you feel it inside you?" he asked. "Moving around?"

A change came over Eric's face: it went still and pale, as though something essential to the function of life had been wrested from him, or had simply run down. He blinked, said nothing.

"You can, can't you." Will brushed the hair back from Eric's forehead. An intimate gesture. A kindness. Eric tried to pull away, but there was nowhere to go. "Is it going to come out through your face? Or do I have to make a hole for it?"

"Go away."

"People think you're such a nice guy," Will said, petting Eric's hair softly. "They don't see you the way I do. They don't see the way your eyes go flat when you're drunk. You're ugly in your heart. *I* can see it." He stared at him there, wasting away in his own bed, crawling with flies and marinating in his own stink. He'd always been ugly inside, and now, finally, anybody could see it. He wanted to drag him through the street, or down to the bar, and hang him from a hook on the wall. He wanted to make it plain to everybody. "Do you have to be dead first? Or will it break you open while you're still alive?"

Eric sobbed. Tears spilled from the corners of his eyes and ran into his hair, his ears. He reached out and clutched Will's hand. He brought it close to his face, almost kissing it. "Please kill me," he said. "Please. I don't want it to come. I don't want to be alive when it happens. I'm scared."

"I wonder what would happen if I called it."

Eric's whimpering stalled. He fixed Will with a look of naked terror.

Will went back into the kitchen and did a little search for a bottle of something, anything to smooth the edges of the experience. He found a third of a bottle of some basement brand rum in the back of one of the cabinets, and walked calmly back into the bedroom, where he sat on the bed by Eric's side and dialed up Garrett's number on his phone.

When the grotesque language began to spill into his ear, he put the phone on speaker, and set it on the mattress. Eric mewled like an animal, curling into himself. Will felt the old, empty ache bestir itself again, and he welcomed it as one would welcome an old friend. They listened, and he drank, for some time. The heat crowded the air out of the room. At some point, when the light sliding through the blinds had taken on a golden color, he ran out of what was in the bottle. It fell to the floor, where it rolled under the bed. Shortly afterwards Eric began to give birth.

His body went rigid on the bed, a thin keening sound slipped through his teeth. Will leaned in close, watching the rupture in his face. It was a blood-rimmed crater into dark precincts. Eric's thin wail interlaced with the cracked slurry of words leaking from the phone, combining to produce a beautiful threnody, a glittering lament that landed in him like hooks.

Thick bone cracked with a shocking sound, and blood spat from Eric's face, splashing in a sudden thick river over his cheek.

Something struggled into the light.

Will felt the presence of it before he could see it. He felt an answer to the long ache. He leaned over Eric's shuddering body, brought his face close. He opened his mouth over the wound, touched his lips to its ragged edges. *Fix me,* he thought. *Please. Make me whole.* He closed his eyes, felt the billowing heat of it. Something moved against his tongue and he sobbed with a terrified gratitude as it probed the roof of his mouth, his teeth and his cheeks. Filling his mouth. He opened wider and gulped it all in, blood leaking from the seal of his lips. Eric began to shriek, repeatedly and in escalating volume, and a host of startled cockroaches scrambled from their lairs, climbing up the walls and rising into the air with their dark, humming wings, a swarm of Christ-bound spirits.

ABOUT THE AUTHOR

Nathan Ballingrud is an American writer of horror and dark fantasy. His first book, the short story collection *North American Lake Monsters*, was published in 2013 by Small Beer Press to great acclaim, including winning the Shirley Jackson Award and being shortlisted for the World Fantasy, British Fantasy, and Bram Stoker awards. He lives in Asheville, NC, with his daughter.